MW00893831

TOBY MAKES A NEW FRIEND

Leo Donaldson

*****

Copyright © 2016 Leo Donaldson
Cover Design and artwork © 2016 Leo Donaldson

All rights reserved

*****

Please note that I use English-(South African) spelling throughout.
You will see doubled letters (focussed), ou's (colour) and 're' (centre)
as well as a few other differences from American spelling.

*****

Toby makes a new friend

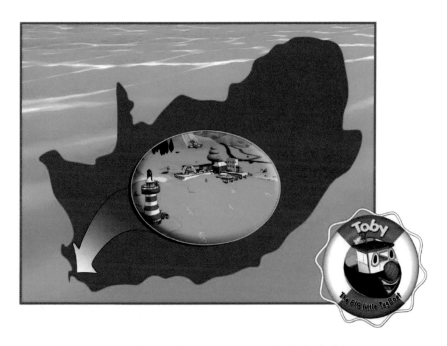

This book is dedicated to my wonderful children,
Jean-Luc and Jess-Leigh, and to Jethro who,
sadly, will never have the joy of reading it.

Andy

Maggie

Toby

Mike Gull

The BIG little TugBoat

Larry-Lorry

Mr. Brightly

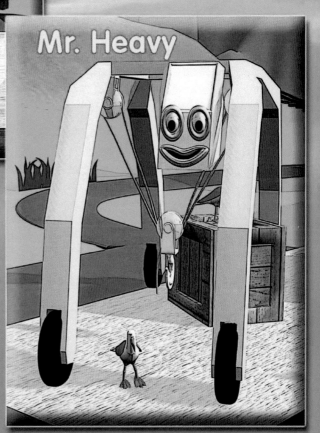

Mr. Heavy

It's a lovely day in the harbour. Toby the tugboat and Maggie the racing yacht are playing with two little sailboats, Skittle and Scant. On the Kalk Bay dock Mr. Heavy and Larry-Lorry are enjoying the morning sun.

In the clear blue sky the seagulls are squawking as they fly, while Andy the little aeroplane is flying playfully in the distance.

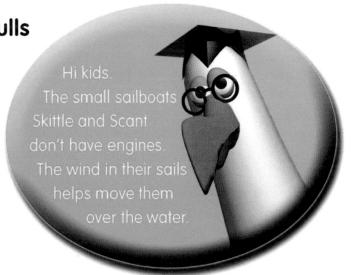

Hi kids.
The small sailboats
Skittle and Scant
don't have engines.
The wind in their sails
helps move them
over the water.

5

The boat friends take a rest from their game.

'Let's play a different game; you always win when we play this one,' Maggie complains to Toby.

The four friends look at one another, each waiting for the others to suggest something.

'Hmm, now let me see. I know, let's have a race!' shouts Toby excitedly.

Maggie smiles broadly. She thinks that's a wonderful idea because she's sure she'll win. It's the one thing she knows she's better at than Toby.

'Okay,' says Maggie, careful not to sound too excited.

'We can race to Mr. Brightly and back again,' adds Toby.

Always ready for fun, Skittle and Scant agree to help.

9

Why do you think Maggie knows she can beat Toby in a race?

'Well, that's quite far. But … okay, it sounds as though it might be fun,' agrees Maggie.

'Right! 1 - 2 - 3 … Go!' calls Toby. Before anybody realises what's happening, he whooshes off as fast as he can go.

'TOBY. COME BACK, TOBY!' Maggie shouts loudly. 'That's not the way to start a race! Everyone must line up together, and wait for the signal,' she explains.

Toby stops and turns around.

Toby is so tired from his dash to Mr. Brightly, he pants, 'Well, you heard me counting. You should also have started when I shouted "Go". So what do you want to do?'

'Someone who isn't taking part in the race should start us off,' suggests Maggie. 'That's the right way to do it, to make sure everything is fair. Let's ask Mr. Heavy if he could do it for us. I'm sure he won't mind.'

They make their way back to the wharf. Toby sails more slowly as he catches his breath.

'Mr. Heavy?' calls Toby. 'Will you please do us a favour?'

'And what would that be, Toby?' replies Mr. Heavy.

'Maggie and I would like to race each other, to Mr. Brightly and back. Could you start the race for us, please?'

I love running races, don't you? It's SO much fun. How fast can you run?

14

'Of course I can do that for you,' smiles Mr. Heavy.

Turning to the little sailboats, Maggie points, 'Skittle? Scant? Will you please form a starting line, from here to over there?'

Skittle and Scant eagerly move into place. Maggie and Toby line up between them.

'Are you ready then?' booms Mr. Heavy in his deep voice. 'Take your marks!'

Toby and Maggie rev their engines in excitement.

'Get set!' Mr. Heavy continues.

Maggie and Toby rev their engines again,

while Skittle and Scant steady themselves as

they wait for the rush of water from Toby and Maggie's start.

Even the seagulls are unusually quiet, waiting anxiously for

the race to begin.

'GO!' shouts Mr. Heavy very loudly.

Engines roar as Toby and Maggie race towards

Mr. Brightly. Poor Skittle and Scant rock back

and forth as they are showered in

waves of water.

I wonder who will win the race? Toby or Maggie? What do you think?

21

Above the boats, the seagulls squawk

and scream with excitement.

On the wharf Mr. Heavy, Larry-Lorry

and a row of seagulls cheer as Maggie

and Toby speed away from them.

'Toby is sure to win this race,' says

Mr. Heavy confidently.

   'I d-don't th-think s-so,' stutters Larry excitedly.

'M-maggie is a r-racing yacht, s-so she's m-much f-faster.

Sh-she will win for s-sure!'

'Perhaps you're right, Larry. Maggie is way ahead of Toby now,' agrees Mr. Heavy. He sounds disappointed.

'B-but, I-look, M-mr. Heavy. It I-looks as th-though T-toby is s-slowing down. In f-fact, h-he seems to have s-stopped!' Larry-Lorry is concerned. Something must be wrong but what can it be?

'I hope he's all right?' says Mr. Heavy,

stretching to take a better look.

'Is th-that s-s-something I see

in the w-water next to T-toby?' asks Larry.

'I see something,' agrees Mr. Heavy,

'but I don't know what it is.

Ooh, I do hope Toby is careful.'

29

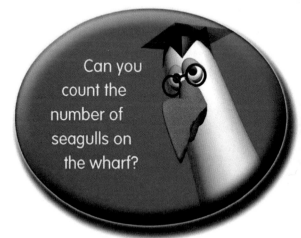

Can you count the number of seagulls on the wharf?

Maggie smiles as she speeds along towards Mr. Brightly. I'm winning, I'm winning, she thinks. She turns back to see where Toby is and her heart sinks.

Toby is no longer racing. What is Toby up to? Is he in trouble? Is he trying to trick her? Maggie turns around and starts to sail back slowly.

'What are you doing, Toby?' calls Maggie. She's a bit cross because she was winning the race.

'Shhhh! Look,' whispers Toby, his eyes fixed on something in the water in front of him.

'What is it?' she asks. She's puzzled by the strange-looking object in the water between herself and Toby.

It looks like ... mmm, well now, let me think ... What do you think it is, kids?

33

Still whispering, Toby says, 'I'm not sure. Let's be careful though, turn off your engine. The noise might frighten it away.'

Maggie drifts curiously towards the strange object. The race now quite forgotten, she also whispers, 'But what is it?'

'I have no idea. I think it's some sort of fish,' replies Toby softly. 'It does look quite cute though, don't you think, Maggie?'

'Hey there, little fellow?' calls Maggie. 'What's your name?'

Suddenly, the creature jumps up out of the water right over Toby.

'My name is Daphne and I'm a dolphin,' she says as she appears out of the water.

'Oh, I know, you're a fish!' exclaims Toby.

Daphne laughs. 'No silly, I'm not a fish, I'm a mammal. Fish have gills and breathe under water. Dolphins don't do that. What are you?' asks Daphne. 'I've never seen a fish that swims on top of the water before.' She looks from Toby to Maggie with a puzzled expression on her face.

Dolphins breathe through a hole on the top of their heads. They have to take a deep breath before going under water.

38

'My name is Toby and I'm a tugboat, not a fish. This is my friend Maggie. She's a motor yacht,' explains Toby as they all start to giggle.

'Pleased to ...'

Toby and Maggie watch in amazement as Daphne disappears, head first into the water. Seconds later, she pops up.

'... meet you,' she says with a smile.

'You can also be my friend. We could play a game in the harbour, if you like,' offers Toby.

'Yippee! That will be fun,' Daphne shouts excitedly. 'Hide and seek is the best game. You can't dive under the water, but I can. You'll have to look really hard to find me!'

Skittle and Scant join in the game. Each agrees to take a turn to find the others. Toby takes the first turn. Maggie, Daphne, and Skittle and Scant find places to hide.

'They're having so much fun,' says Mr. Heavy,

as he and Larry-Lorry watch Toby, Maggie, Skittle and Scant

playing in the water with their new friend, Daphne.

'S-s-sometimes I w-wish I could j-join them in the water,'

sighs Larry-Lorry.

The sky is becoming dark quickly.

Daphne waves goodbye to her new friends. 'I promise I'll be back tomorrow,' she says. 'I must go now. Mummy will be worried about me.'

'Goodbye, Daphne,' Toby yawns happily.

Now that was an exciting day! Visit us next time for more fun and adventure. Good night, kids.

'See you soon,' sighs Maggie, almost too tired to keep her eyelids open.

Soon, all of the friends are fast asleep and in dreamland.

46

Made in the USA
San Bernardino, CA
30 March 2020

66550036R00029